SHE LEARNS TO FLY-AGAIN

SHE LEARNS TO FLY-AGAIN

RITU SETHI

SHE LEARNS TO FLY-AGAIN

iUniverse books may be ordered through booksellers or by contacting:

iUniverse
1663 Liberty Drive
Bloomington, IN 47403
www.iuniverse.com
1-800-Authors (1-800-288-4677)

ISBN: 978-1-5320-8841-4 (sc)
ISBN: 978-1-5320-8842-1 (e)

Library of Congress Control Number: 2019919382

Print information available on the last page.

iUniverse rev. date: 11/27/2019

CHAPTER

S ITTING ON HELLO SITTING ON HER FAVORITE WICKER CHAIR CRADLING
her favorite mug of coffee she looked outside the big patio glass
door. Early in the morning fresh dewdrops sat on the edge off the
leaves outside. She looked to the dewdrops you've drops she's saw a
bunch of kids laughing and kicking making the way to the bus.

Ragani was soon transported to the past, this is much she saw the
faces of her kids sh SH I V, Arjun and Arya her the precious bundles
of joy. She was transported through the rainbow to they was running
by playing and laughing their faces turn pink from the shirt actually
from the sheer joy and laughter Richfield around them. She saw gets
climbed a bus I'm going off to school and hi daily grind started being

the mother of three at the young age of 25 what's no easy task but she was young and for love energy thinking back I think she got the energy from her kids she had a lot of growing up to do and she didn't and she did it with her kids. The Five of them all grew up together.

CHAPTER

Ragani life in USA

S HE OPENED THE DOOR WITH THE KEYS HER SISTER IN LAW HAD GIVEN her. With hands shaking, she entered the two-bedroom apartment. She took a step in, closed the door firmly almost like saying a firm goodbye to the past. She walked in the dim light slowly switching the lights on. As she moved, she was seeing her future ahead. She slowly picked up the clothes that lay all over the sofa, the carpet, the floor, the bed and hanging on the doors. Dishes scattered everywhere dirty glasses, dishes, and dirty mugs plates. There was a slight stink coming from everything. Slowly she started picking up the clothes and dirty dishes not knowing what to do she entered the kitchen and slowly started washing the dishes, rubbing hard on them as I she wanted to rub the entire scene.

Everyone took another sip of the coffee as she reflected. She had never washed dirty dishes learnt to cook clean and wash clothes

Everyone thought that she liked school, took dance lessons she took up guitar she learnt to play. She should have learnt how to do dirty dishes in fact reflecting back her mind asked her shouldn't it be mandatory for all kids to learn these household chores because life ultimately teaches you one way or the other. Unless you can afford a personal maid to send with your daughter especially if you are getting them married off outside India.

Anyone saw a small perfume bottle of 'Brut' the name still sticks in her mind and when she is shopping, she quickly removes her eyes from the bottle. But the smell in the 2 bedroom apartment was overwhelming so she took the small bottle of Brut and sprayed a little in of it in every nook and corner making sure she was not using too much scared of Shivans reaction.

Her suitcases still lay closed not knowing where she and her stuff belonged. Her mother in law had kept all her jewellery the personal gifts given by people close to her heart nothing belonged to her.

She opened her suitcase and broke down into tears. The feelings, which were bottled up so far, could no longer be stopped. She cries till there were no more tears left. After the long fight and after all that happened afterwards left her empty. Nothing seemed to be hers. She took a quick shower changed and just waited for what lay ahead.

It was almost a day with no food in the house she curled up into a ball and fell asleep. She woke up with a sudden noise.

Shivam her so-called husband had entered the apartment.

She did not know how to greet him. He was but a stranger.

And his reaction when anyone was at her sisters left a very sour taste in her mouth.

Putting on some makeup to hide her tears she got ready to greet him. She said to him barely a hello. Shivam swept her in his arms and what Ranjana feared all along happened. He raped her, there were no kisses or hugs, no, I love you, and I have missed you. This time Ranjana broke into tears. Shivam was taken aback and asked her and Ranjana looking for some comfort cling to him and cried. How could not understand why.

Shivam and Ranjana

So now, Shivam took a flight of stairs where there was a common washer and dryer. Now Shivam had a personal maid whom he could have had sex with whenever he wanted, who would cook and clean and do the laundry. Ranjana had the $800, which her parents had given her.

So started the daily routine he nudged her in the morning to get up and make him bed. Ranjana was like a robot and did as she was told. She had never cooked in her entire life.

But life teaches you the hardest lessons. Yes, of course Ranjaan knew how to prepare special dishes likes cakes and fancy appetizers. But that was not real food. She started cooking at 11 am and tasted the food, which tasted like garbage so she threw it away and started cooking again. This process would go on till 5pm for a month when she would taste and try to improve.

Shivam seemed to be a very insensitive man. He would throw the chapatis like a flying saucer and tell Ranjana- you eat it. Finally,

Ranjana found perfect method- a lid of a container. So after making maps of various countries she would cut them in a perfect round.

Shivam was doing his fellowship. Rita sat in the apartment. Taking the bus to buy groceries in the cold all 5 feet of he walked to the bus stand and told there waiting for the bus.

Shivam gave her exactly $100 to buy groceries for the entire month. She counted and recounted the money. Could she buy anything she liked? Of course, not, she had to buy chicken nuggets and Hagen daz ice cream for Shivam who would come late and gulp down the chicken nuggets while Rita stared and watched the one chicken nugget hoping in vain that he would at least offer her one.

Slowly she moved and in the bathroom turned on the tap and cried her eyes out. She could not believe that she was in a situation from which there was no escape. Rita, who had been very independent, was now dependent on a person for a piece of chicken. She never too her parents though. Why? Because her older sister was dealing with a tough situation and she felt that she should deal with whatever came her way. That was a major fault on her part because all chains of communication she had with her family were slowly breaking down.

Suddenly, a bad maid broke off her chain of thoughts. Are you coming in to clean up? Wiping away her tears and facing a glaring face, she came out apologizing.

Shivam gave her a dirty look and went into the bedroom.

Rajaani slowly cleaned up taking her time and hoping he would be fast asleep when she entered the bedroom. There was another role she had to play. The role of a whore. But Shivam would be wide-awake. To Ranjana it seemed that she did enjoy the physical relationship with Shivam but slowly she was getting more and more mentally detached from Shivam.

Then came the stork, and then came the mother in law.

Shivam and Rajaani did not want babies yet so she was using birth control. Every time her mother in law called it was the same question, Are you pregnant yet? She was not of course. Was something wrong with her? Her mother in law shouting would lay- and what was more stranger was the fact that Shivam never told his mother that he did not want a child yet. So by proxy, something was wrong with Ranjani, as is assumed by all Indian mother in laws.

Six or 7 months down the marriage, ranjaani was pregnant, so mother in law dearest decided to come down and stay. Shivam was a mama's boy. He kept quiet and was very happy. Ranjaani on the other hand was very disturbed because she had lived with the so-called mother in law and was terrified. It was anger and frustration all in a package.

Shivam had a family function so that became a pretext. Ranjani begged and begged Shivam to let her mother come for her first pregnancy. What was the answer- but of course a big no.

Ranjani slowly began to feel depressed. She had a very difficult pregnancy, many times Drs suggested complete bedrest, but really who was there for Rajaani to cook, clean and do the laundry, which was a flight of steps. Shivam was of no help and neither was the dragon lady.

Ranjani took the bus for her regular checkups every two weeks on the bus to the drs clinic.

On one such cold winter morning Ranjani went for another checkup and the Dr couldn't find the heartbeat of the baby.

Dr Kristina made her walk up and downside made her drink water, but still no heartbeat. Ranjani by this time was going thru a physical and emotional anguish.

She was scared when the Dr told her to go get admitted to the hospital. So Ranjani dragged herself to the hospital and got herself admitted. Those were the days there were no cell phones, just the big black ones came out. She called Shivam and called her sister in law.

The Dr before they came made a major blunder; they induced Ranjani instead of doing a C-section. And taking the baby out Rajani for some reason developed high fever of 102 and 103. With that she had no strength in her to push she lost consciousness at one stage. 26 Hrs go labor and finally the baby came out all blue and not breathing. They rushed him to the children ward, gave him CPR and put the baby in an oxygen tent with tiny tubes monitoring him.

Ranjani was now bleeding extensively and the Drs had to rush her to the operating theatre. 9 months with repeated ultrasounds Dr Kristen has missed the fact that Ranjani had a condition called placenta acreata. Where the placenta grows outside rather than in the uterus.

The baby therefore could not get enough nutrition.

By now, Dr Kristen had called 2 others Drs, Dr John and Dr Rab.

In the operating theatre, Rajani kept on pleading with the Dr to meet Shivam and her newborn. The 3 Drs wanted to give Rajani anesthesia and Rajani was absolute sure she did not want get it.

She wanted to talk to Shivam and ask if the baby is doing OK.

Rajani vividly recalls Dr yelling: You want to die Rajani for someone who has not even come to see you even once?

Finally, Shivam came and said he a blunt voice, what do you want the baby is not doing well.

It never occurred to him that if Rajani lived they would be able to have another baby. But being Mama's boy being more important than a male child who had taken a few breaths.

The Drs did the procedure, which took 2 hours.

When Rajani opened her eyes, she was in the room. The baby was in the oxygen tent. What as frustrating and amusing was that the mother in law and Shivam without consulting Rajani had given the baby a name: Sumit, Rajani wanted to name the child but was neither asked nor consulted. She was very upset and rightfully so. There was no energy left in her with 26 hrs of labor pains and 2 hrs of procedure. She was exhausted and had no energy left. Two days in the hospital with a hemoglobin of 7 she was discharged but her heart was in the hospital. Reaching the apartment Shivams first words were "you have to lose weight". Rajani went to the bathroom and cried and cried til she had no tears left. Exhausted as she was, she just went to bed.

Getting up the next morning early to be with her newborn thanking the lucky stars for being the mother she was the only one allowed to touch the baby and hold his tiny hands. He was so fragile and Rajani was scared she would hurt him. She held him like the most expensive piece of bone china. Even more unfortunate Rajani could not feed him because the baby had no strength to suck. Rajani could not produce milk as hard as she tried. Rajani' s baby was in the hospital for good month or so. Everyday Rajani went to the hospital to hold Sumit to kiss him and see his tiny fingers. One day he held Rajanis fingers and Rajani was overcome with a bunch of emotions. She kept on telling the nurse see he is holding my finger. The nurse said but of course, you are his mother. What a delight it was with his big black eyes he looked at Rajani and she burst into tears. He was the most precious procreation and Rajani dreaded the day he would be discharged. He was placed in a heart monitor and placed in the car seat. Shivam and the mother in law came to take Rajani and Sumit home or more than Rajani takes Sumit home.

Rajani knew by now that if it had come to a point if the drs had said we can save either the mother's life or the child's life their reply would have been the child life. As days passed by Rajani moved to another room because Sumit heart monitor would go off even if he moved and Rajani would get up shake the baby and make sure he was breathing. Rajani was very naive and did not know how to change diapers. One night Sumit pooped and Rajani took him to the changing table where Shivam slept so as not to wake him up Rajani tried to do it herself.

Well what a hilarious scene it was Sumit kicking with his tiny legs and arms was full of poop. Rajani herself was full of poop; in the hospital, the nurses changed the diapers. Sumit and Rajani were both howling now. Shivam got up, switched the light on and burst out laughing at the scene before him. I'm front of him, he got up told Rajani to go take a shower and he cleaned Sumit up. Rajani by now was laughing too, it was a kodak moment.

So after both of them cleaned up Shivam kissed the little bundle of joy. Rajani wished Shivam would always be with her like this loving, laughing Shivam whom she had grown to love. Maybe it was just Shivam or maybe it was just Sumit and not ragini.

By now, Rajani knew the mother in law was of no help what so ever. So in the daytime she got very little sleep with Sumit at night when she got up she did all the chores cooking cleaning and laundry. This was her work and she expected nothing from anyone. Rajani broke down when she came to know that all the blankets she had make for her grandchild the tiny socks and caps had disappeared. She questioned Shivam who clearly said that since his mother did not want them they drove to good will and donated the stuff without asking me, Rajani. Rajani could never forgive or forget this gesture. By now, Rajani had developed a total dislike for her mother in law.

Shivam mother finally left and what a relief it was Ragani and Shivam were now enjoying each other's company. They actually talked and prayed with Sumit each day they saw him grow. Their concerns for him seemed to be unfounded. A kid who could jump out of his crib at 4 months could conquer it all.

He never crawled at 6 months and he was walking and holding on to the chairs and tables. What s bundle of joy Sumit was to all of us. He seemed to bring Sumit and Rajani closer.

Life seemed so much better and happier though Rajani had to work a lot she did not seem to mind it. To her it now seemed to be part of life with a grain of salt in it.

Rajani seemed to be living in fool's paradise because she failed to recognize that in between the stolen moments to pizza hut or watching 'pretty woman' there was a trembling underground almost like a dormant lava or earthquake

Rajani who was a much happier person now was full of life and jest. For now, she had the gift of all. She had her baby Sumit.

Her mother in law this time came back with the father in law in tow.

One day when Rajani was driving to the new houses, they had just bought she felt the severe urge to eat chicken nuggets. She drove to McDonalds and bought 6 pieces of chicken nuggets she felt so hungry that she was gulping them down as if she had never had them before. As soon as she was done gobbling down the chicken nuggets, she threw up right away. Rajani knew something was wrong. She drove to the nearest Walgreens and picked up a home testing kit to detect pregnancy. She rushed back to the apartment with Sumit still in her arms, went into the bathroom and completed the pregnancy test. Lo and behold she all relics... Required to read the thing but also triggered like beat commitment forms know this when you yet astronomy or circular feeling fish his eye-opener she told me you're coming. It should muscle faces florescent strong smelling and smelling you do again. Rajani became pale as if all the blood had been drained from her body. She called Shivam to let him know and Shivam was like' how is this possible'. Rajani thought what an idiot this guy is. How does he not know how Rajani got pregnant? Rajani going thru postpartum depression had to stop the pregnancy, Sumit was her dearest passion and she did not want to ham her unborn child so she stopped the depression medications.

Rajani begged Shivam to get her mother to come this time to help, but no- his mother dearest was to come again. Rajani was very disappointed with Shivam because the closeness they were having and enjoying would soon disappear. Rajani used to feel very sleepy during the pregnancy but she had Sumit who was like an energizer bunny. He started talking very early and Rajani and he used to sing and dance to 'fishy in the tank' and 'barney' tapes.

Then of course, the mother in law came and said to Rajani this is my son's house- that let Rajani to think well where her house was? Was it Shivanis, her parents where did she belong?

There was a big turmoil going on in her mind, who was she? Just Mrs so & so, just summit's mother? It seemed that she had lost her own identity. Every day she prayed hard asking herself "who am I?"

She was 8 months pregnant and she was washing the dishes. At night after dinner, she started putting the dishes in the dishwasher and she heard her mother in laws voice: why are you putting the dishes in the dishwasher-, you are wasting my son's money. Rajani was taken aback- her sons dish washer? Was it true or not? Shivam who was sitting right there did not say a word. Here was a high on month lady. Rajani was 25 yrs old with a sister in law and all these people. Shivam, the mother in law, father in law cracking all these jokes and laughing. Rajani actually called raps by her friends and Shivam was by reaching a hailing point want to stop all these people.

Wondering what kind of people they are she had more and more disappointment and cruelty coming her way. She was now seen as a maid to cook, clean and serve and become a whore at night. One day at dinner Rajani asked if she could make Indian tortillas before hand and out came the mother in laws voice- no we will have fresh ones. With tears rolling down her cheeks and 8 months pregnant Rags served hot chappties to them. Not one of them asked her; why don't you eat? It was hurtful most to her, Raps with her back hurting barely had the energy to sit down and eat. The only force that made her eat was her unborn baby she knew the baby needed the food so she forced herself tonormally was very doable doing it to New York on Sunday. No-one asked her asked her whether she was hungry Nor did they ask her. Raps has become a very different person from the cheerful laughing person an extrovert full of life had become an angry frustrated and depressed person.

She had no support system if her friends called in Anjali and Seems had become his support. Everyone that called -her mother in law picked up the phone from the other end and would listen to every word. Everything was bring monitored by her mother in law. The interference was slowly killing Rajani.

So Shivam now started a different game plan. He has 5 siblings, 3 female and 2 male.

Sandy, Aisha, Shivani, Blossom and Sachin.

Sandy lived the closest. So from work Shivam would go directly to Sandy's house. Both mother in law and father in law were there already. What they planned and talked about Rajani was kept out of, it was like the secret 4 Enid Blyton books that we read as children.

One day ragini called Shivam and asked him when was he coming home? He answered he was attending a meeting and would be late. Rajani heard a voice from behind. She by now was not the timid quiet Rajani anymore.

She walked up to sandy house and she saw shivams car parked right there on the drive way. So as not to make a scene she kept quiet and walked back. Inside she was again having a deep hatred for the lies and choices this family was.

Rajani by now was getting convinced that these people will never speak the truth they were just a bunch of sick individuals and the only reason Shivam married ragini was to reproduce.

Rajani gathered up the courage to ask Shivam point blank- why did you lie to me when all this time you were at sandy house?

I was waiting for you. Out came the reply- so now you are spying on me? Ragini told him she was not spying but now Shivam was upset. Not because he had done something wrong but because his lie was caught.

A guilty conscious person never lies- they don't have the courage to face the truth- they try to make it sound it was the other persons fault.

So whatever the conspiracy theory continued, Rajani was getting more and more depressed day by day. She has a husband who never stood up for her. her mother in law and father in law added with a sister in law. The only saving grace was her kids whom she adored. Life was getting to be frustrating. Tired small babies no one to talk to was slowly but steadily taking toll on ragini.

Shivam was the biggest disappointment, the one person who should have supported her was supporting everyone but her. Life was tough, trying Ragini's patience.

Shivam found a new job and they bought a house. Ragini even though pregnant kept going from cleaning the new house to putting paper lining in the drawers. The next pregnancy was way easy and she had a beautiful boy. Now it was getting tough for Ragini to manage the house, 2 boys and all the chores. Of course mother in law came in too. There was stuffed toy of snoopy he dog. Both the kids laughed when they looked at him. Ragini placed him a place on the kitchen counter but for her mother in law it was an issue. She always turned her face away. why? It was sons house and she would do things her way. However much Ragini tried to explain that it makes the kids happy, she would not have it and would not listed.

Sandy with blossom and reaching. The lady was like no no Dr. so anyway just during right believing it months five and was advised by the doctor not to fly the tenacity of Sharon's family was incredible they told Sharon to leave drag me alone and come to New York Sharon was already to go he called a frog and his doctrine asked her whether it would be okay for him to leave her during her pregnancy next as a thoughts to buy revenue she was curled up in the chair tears rolling down her cheeks. It was getting dark so she closed the door, came inside as if she was closing the bad memories from coming into the new dwelling. So Rodney by now kind of understood what was going around. She knew she was alone and shoot so was her struggle. She had heard of so many tales like these and endeavor to her astonishment. The same events were getting played here in America. Sharon wanted her to play 412 roles. Sufficiently, the role of the perfect American graduate on the role of perfect undergraduate. Frog made was a struggle because she could never understand which role he wanted her to play and how anyway life continued at its usual pace. She loved to play with her two boys and then she discovered she was pregnant again. She was not scared that she would have three little ones. All she was more scared off was the mother how would come again. She longed for a baby girl knowing the fact she decided not to tell Sharon as always. She used to go to the doctor's appointment alone with Sumit and Kabir with her so she pretty much was able to hide it from Siobhan for a good three months after that he found out only because Rodney was wearing such loose floats marketing was wearing such loose clothes knowing Dragon Amy meal – rugby was a type a personality she always used to dress well so this was definitely not her style so he asked her what was up and Rodney said I think I am pregnant John jumped out of the van and asked her Rodney pretended she did not know and I just found out Sharon was totally taken aback he was asking how long and ripening knowing perfectly well for how long said she did not know so this time Siobhan decided to go to the doctor with her and find out the bargaining was already three months pregnant he was hopping mad for now there was no chance of aborting the child this song four days together and finally realized that whatever will be will be so finally he began to really enjoy being a full-time dad. It did her Dragon a pretty bad but for his kid so meet in February was the perfect father so it was a pretty fussy eater social bounty Shiva monogamy would sit outside on the patio and sing and dance and did all kinds of tricks to make and eat Little Kabir was satisfied with a bottle of milk when Kabir was born little Smith would turn Stan on the playpen and kept on saying Mimi loudly my baby my baby there was no sibling rivalry between the two strange as it may sound they became the best friends Smith and Covey were very interested by Siobhan's shaving but they would climb on the bathroom countertop and Sharon had to put foam on dad and use the backside of the razor they were flourishing in the positive happy environment but things change the mother-in-law came and interfered in every single thing when Sharon Sharon would come home from work Rodney used to take water for him Wallace took his shoes off asking him I was a stay the mother-in-law would scream from the living room and say stop bothering him is just come home from work leapfrogging he was literally taken a back for she was just a few minutes with Sharon Cheryl's mother called could not digested she kept on coloring rugby on every given opportunity and Sharon dearest could never tell his mother the please give us some more time alone these little tantrums that she was throwing was slowly taking a toll on progeny she was getting more and more depressed and going in on a very dark song she wondered till when and why she was taking these insults and this behavior because Rodney was pregnant she had to stop the anti-depressive mood Sean's mother started making more Indian snacks for daughters dearest who was also pregnant and could not make them because she couldn't tolerate the smell Rodney was nauseous at the very spell and she kept on pleading Sharon and his mother to stop it but didn't stop her no it was winter and Rodney put on a long quote to go outside the house because she could not tolerate the smell another shiver monogamous mother came out once to take five month drag me inside why was this happening where had she gone wrong finding no answer shivering in the cold hard to realize the fact that Sherm would not support her emotionally or otherwise she was alone in this matter Rodney was terribly hurt and angry at Sharon and his mother 20 minutes later she went inside got fed the kids and went to sleep she knew that she was pregnant and should eat proper meals with no one really cared putting the boys to bed and singing a lullaby was something that calmed her my precious kids go to sleep the winds blew slowly for my precious babies are going to sleep flyby annuals and put them to sleep stay quiet not a sound should come for my precious babies are born sleep on angels help me put my babies to sleep Riley would sing for them holding the little hands it was so coming for her for Agni it was like the healing process Simeon would tell her to keep singing what a beautiful picture was writing wish wish that everything should freeze these moments rugby had made up her mind that this pregnancy she would insist she would take up anyway now that her in-laws were busy with family and her pregnancy so she went to send this place raggedy was feeling pleased Symington community started going to prekindergarten and preschool the school is a good 30 minute drive so she drove for a good one hour in between she would work quick for the evening do the laundry clean up the house take a short nap exercise and drive back to pick the kids up Rodney felt blessed when she went to pick them up later the boys would run with hands outstretched and mommy mommy Riley felt lesson from there hugs came out the power that she could conquer it all the 3 Office Would Dr. back singing and talking as to what new things they did in school how precious while these moments for our date was a lifetime for her sanity and peace of mind Rodney had a pretty easy delivery this time and out came a baby girl Brian renamed her Annika which means Conestoga Rodney came on the next day and some even computed not digested too well for them she was a baby homemade loud singing songs and was further crying gradually came weapons that Annika was staying in the house for good firstly for arguing she could not feel the babies because she produce no milk it all boiled to the fact that Dragon had a malnourished body and Little therefore no milk however I really missed her mother's house with the little ones just running with baby Amico crawling behind her brother sometimes they would get pretty upset and complained why she always following us Dragon a try to best explain it to both Smith and Kabir that she is your beautiful sister and she follows you because she wants to play with you but it fell on deaf ears and after were dragging me heard the song with some eight into their room and Amica trying DeLong the deer in trying to go inside Brandon tried to move to another room because she will need her to sleep Rodney had requested and beg for rocking chair but for Rodney it was a big no for his sister a big yes Dragon tried to explain to Sharon that she really needed it because it was very difficult for her to sleep on a folding bed which was old and drag me back was giving away and Annika would refuse to sleep in a crib and needed to be fed at night but there were these years that would pitch and so there were no more Sonny Karami would eventually both and up on the folding bed his Majesty wanted venting the morning so Rodney would drive herself down to make a study take it to his room soon the boys would be up in Dragon he could get them ready for school make breakfast for the three she wants a neat and Kabir I make I would be fully awake by now crying to her lungs out an arts bracketing have to bundled her up to drive the boys to school it was a tough job for her and she would crush one day in the meanwhile Sean's mom got really sick and could not take care of herself so it was decided by the siblings that she would stitch a woman's house she wants mother fell sick in the meanwhile so as usual the five siblings decided that she would stay with Sharon why and for what reason Rodney was not consulted Soraya Nino had three little ones running around taking them for swimming classes and other activities and already a full-time job then she wondered if she could handle it but from her tiny former 53 120 pounds she was getting both emotionally and physically hard Bradley remembered today as clear as when she had a first breakdown Sharon and baby are you were not easy to take your off she handled them give them a bottle of milk and they would drink and fall asleep when she was cooking standing it was 2:30 PM Arachne had not slept yet and little pardon asking crying if he wanted his mother to feed him Ragnar stopped working and culture them back home take care for parents and siblings I will not do it imagine her taking cure-all for mother's frustration when she could not feed our kids frustrated yes that it was with tears drops and crying with our German she grab something from the refrigerator and made herself a hot cup of coffee picked up her kids shave Arjun Arianna and when upstairs to the kids bedroom to sleep then she broke down all of her shaking from anger and frustration Hungary all rolled spiral down into each other she fed her little Arjun all the time thinking what a horrible mother she was when she could not feed him Sharon in the meanwhile handing his patients to those partner came over he had three siblings Dragon enjoyed being a mother so much semi thin conveyor were like best friends and Annika was like a lost puppy following them whenever they went many times they would here are her either Kobe or Smith young mom can you stop her from following us Rodney would yell back no I cannot the funny thing was a frightening asked Re: estimate and career would come back and told writing. Scolding the baby to so little why are you scolding her and Annika was full advantage of her support she would look at bargaining with puppy eyes Rodney with put façade of a strict mother would melt and give all three a big hug the back-and-forth from school asking them what happened all the time went around the baby and fake trying to gain some attention it was hilarious as Dragon he thought about it the boys now knowing why Annika was crying what time together figure figure not knowing whether boys were saying Annika would laugh and clap your hands thinking about what Kabir was going to do one day submit came up with her and asked Ragan he is an Fabian equipped to fat her cheeks are so chubby we should put her on a diet a first grader talking about diet while this little champ was growing up fast in this world where every second it's talking about going on a diet the TV ads flashing about this diet and that diet it was sure sometime to compare herself before telling Simi then explained it is her support he sees as fact is just some fat that Annika could do he listened and just told Ron Jenae make sure she doesn't eat more when she asked him why he was so concerned his reply was because you do not want to have a fat sister the imagination and the confusion the frog me thinking what are we teaching our kids when they should be talking about friends and games nice to me. About dieting

Rajani had to move to another room because Shivam needed to

sleep. Rajani had requested and begged for a rocking chair but for rajaani it was a big no, for his sister it was a big yes.

Rajani tried o=to explain to Shivam she really needed it because it was very difficult for her to sleep on a folding bed which was old and rajanis back was giving away and Anika would refuse to sleep in a crib and needed to be fed at night, but where were the ears that would listen to her? There were none. So Anika and Rajani eventually both end up on the folding bed.

His majesty wanted bed tea in the morning so Rajani would drag herself down to make his tea and take it to the room, soon the boys would be up and Rajani would get them ready for school make breakfast for the 3 Shivam, Sumit and Kabir. Anika would be awake by now crying her lungs out and Ragini had to bundle her up to drive the boys to school. It was a tough job and she knew she would crash one day.

In the meanwhile Shivam mom got really sick and cound not take care of herself. So it was decided by the siblings that she would stay at Shivams house.

Shivam mother fell sick in the meanwhile. As usual the 5 siblings decided that she would stay with Shivam. Why and for what reason Rajani was not consulted?

Rajani had 3 little ones running around and was busy with taking them for swimming classes and other activities that were a full time jobs. This she wondered if she could handle it. But her very tiny form of 5.3 and 120 pounds but she was getting exhausted emotionally and physically.

Rajani remembered the day clearly when she had her first breakdown. Shivam was with arya and she handed him a bottle of milk. They would drink and fall asleep and while she was cooking and standing up.

It was 2.30 pm and Rajani had not eaten yet. Little arya started crying she wanted her mother to feed her. Rajani stopped cooking and called Shivam. She asked him to come home and take care of his parents and siblings. She was unable to do it at that time. Imagine a mothers frustration when she cannot even feed her own kids. Frustrated yes that was it, she was crying with little arya she grabbed something from the refrigerator and made herself a cup of coffee. Picked up all her 2 kids, Sumit, Kabir and Arya and went into the kids bedroom and closed the door. She then broke down her hands shaking from anger, frustration and hunger all rolled into each other.

She fed her little arya all the time thinking what a horrible mother she was when she couldn't even feed her.

Shivam meanwhile was handling his patients over to his partner.

Rajani enjoyed being a mother as much as possible and was happy they were part of her life. Sumit and Kabir were best friends and Arya was like a lost puppy following them wherever they went. Many a time she would hear from Kabir or Sumit Maa can you stop her from following us. And Rajani would yell back, No I cannot.

The funny thing was that if rjaani scolded arya, Kabir and Sumit would come and tell Rajani to 'stop scolding the baby'.

Arya took full advantage of her brothers support, and would look at Rajani with puppy eyes.

Rajani would put up a facade of being a strict mother would melt and give all 3 of them big hugs.

Rajani was in a different world. A world in which no one was allowed to enter.

The back and forth from school asking them what has happened all the chatter went around where baby arya reasoned and put fake crying to gain some attention. It was hilarious as Rajani thought about it.

The boys now knowing why arya was crying would chime together faker faker arya is a faker.

Never knowing what the boys were saying arya would laugh and clap her hands thinking that sumit and kabir were singing to her.

One day kabir came up and said isn't arya fat? Why are her cheeks so chubby? Should we put her on a diet? A first grader talking about diet? Wow the little champ was growing up fast. In this world where everyone and very few seconds there are ads about this diet and that diet, Rajani decided to compose herself and before telling summit that what he sees as fat is just baby fat and sure enough arya would lose it too.

He listened and said to make sure that she would lose it because he did not want a fat sister. The imagination and discussion left Rajani thinking what are we teaching our kids when they should be talking about games and friends. My son sumit was talking about dieting.

Then 9/11 happened. It was Rajani schedule to drop the kids off in pre school and one off in third grade. She would go home and make herself a hot cup of chai and watch TV and news for 40 to 60 minutes. She switched the TV on and they were showing the first plane crash into the twin towers. They she saw the second plane come up, by that time she had taken off her shoes and just sat in the lazy boy. Her eyes were glued to the TV.

She could hear people crying for help. All cell phones had been switched off. The bodies that the day care that was there.

Rajani was in a trance and called Shivam brother Anisha and brother Sachin were both working there. While trying to contact them for 10 to 15 minutes no news came of them. Shivam tried calling to ask what had happened. No answers came our way that day.

Rajani after seeing the news segment called the school and told them she wanted to pick up her kids and know that they would be safe at home. Unfortunately many shootings were happening in schools and killing kids for no reason. For sure America was becoming a more violent place.

So now Rajamani was teaching her kids what to do if a gun man enters the classroom hide under the table and do not make any noise.

The real thought of some day something like this really happening in the school and what would she do?

This is a new America where there are new incidents every day.

Rajani' s world revolved around Sumit, Kabir and Arya.

Rajani wondered if Shivam could ever be a good husband?

He never asked Rajani how she was feeling. What did she need that was never asked. Rajani longed for a hug or a little i love you message. Rajani realised in the scheme things she was alone and this was how it was meant to be.

Shivams mother was not feeling very well. The 5 siblings Sandy, Aisha, Blossom and Sachin decided that their mother was going to stay with Shivam and Rajani.

For Rajani that was not the issue. The issue was since she was the one who would be taking care of shivas mother she should have at least been a part of the decision making. Suprisingly none of the 5 siblings were thinking about that and if they did not, it was Shivam himself who should have included her in the process.

Rajani knew this was going to affect her marriage and kids. She must have cried herself to sleep as the pillow was damp in the morning when she woke up. She said her prayers and went on like a zombie to make Shivam his tea. Soon the kids would wake up and her say would start.

So Shivams mother came and she looked quite pale.

Whatever the illness was it was going to affect her small world. With his mother came the package of Sandy, Aisha, Blossom and Sachin. Aisha decided to stay. Sandy was already there.

Rajani who was attach to her Maa knew how they would be faking. But at the same time she wished they would help her in the household chores. Rajani had her hands full with her 3 musketeers and the household chores. Done with laundry and everything Aisha just sat with her mother. It was rajanis job to cook clean and do everything. She would not even get the cup of tea that Rajani had made downstairs. Rajani was slowly but surely getting frustrated by all of them including Shivam. Rajani;s father in law decided to fly from india. Rajani went to pick him up. He had the audacity to tell Rajani that it was because of her that his wife was sick. Really thought Rajani, if it was high BP she could understand. But just like that out of the blue she was responsible? She was the one who should be hanged. Rajani kept quiet but was fuming inside.

They had to do some tests on her mother in law. Rajani was the one taking her for all the appointments. No gratitude from anyone but for snide remarks. If it was not for her 3 kids she would have walked out. But Sumit, Kabir and Arya were too little to understand her plight. Only person was her friend Rebecca and Renu who really knew what she was really going through.

It seemed to her that life had come to a standstill. She did not call her parents-because what would they do sitting in India?

Her Maa had the intuition that something was wrong. One day she called Rajani- and Rajani said really Maa everything was fine.

It would be of no use if she told her sole story, Rajani by not sharing was doing a big disservice to herself, because one can keep things bottled up the bottle would burst one day that was for sure.

With Sandy, Aisha, Blossom and Sachin Rajani was running on no fuel for herself because she was cooking for more people with different demands who never had the courtesy to offer any help whatsoever. These people were all older than Rajani. Rajani was astonished and wondered are there people who call themselves sophisticated ? Carrying a Gucci bag does not make sophisticated nor does their accent. What makes a person sophisticated is their behaviour which was not there. There behaviour to be honest was of illiterate people who have absolutely no manners and did not care a jack shit about their behaviour. Leaving dirty cups, plates only makes one a dirty unwanted guest, nothing more. These people were exactly that. They were doing nothing yet expected everything.

Shivam by the time he came home was so tired that Rajani felt it was useless talking to him about anything. He was working full time, coming home to a sick mother and was very tired.

Rajani felt it would only increase his tension and she did not want that to happen. There was no point in taking about his past behavior that she had been accustomed to. She knew he would never support her, for him blood relationships came first and Rajani was sure not one of them. The problem with the family was that they had never experienced an extended family. For Rajani her cousins were always there for support She never remembered being alone for any festival.

be it Dewali, Holi or anything else. She only remembers the always full house with cousins coming in and out for every little festival.

Thinking about those days brought a smile to her face.

She remembered one holi, a festival of colours. They were all together and one of the cousins got some opium. It is something very much known in the Indian culture and it is called bhang. So they mixed it in a sweet and gave it to the other cousins who unknowingly ate it. The smile came across rajanis face thinking about it. Because her cousin Raj lay flat in the grass screaming I am stuck, I am stuck. I cannot get up. Hence it was really funny lil 2 other cousins Krish and Prem actually picked him up and thru him in a tank full of water. Raj got out of the water and started asking Krish and Prem why the hell they thru him in the water? What great days those were!

For Diwali, we were either at their Badey Papa(fathers older brothers) place or they came over to our place.

It was not just about bursting fire crackers, it was more than that. It was about spending time together, cracking jokes while their mothers prepared all kinds of goodies at home. Rajani still remembers her grandmothers instructions about what was to be done.

Rajani' s grandmother was really a class apart. She would not let anyone sit on her bed. we being the kids, we would purposely do it. She would retaliate by the choicest curses she knew. To us it did not matter. We were what we were, and she was what she was!

Both parties knew the rule of the game and could not think of anything but play their parts. Rajani kept on stacking dishes in the dishwasher oil her trans was broken by a loud yell.

'Rajani' the voice of Sandy, the glass in her hand fell down and shattered.

As she picked up each piece of shattered glass she thought they were almost like her life, she picked up each piece of glass gathering them together with a broom so that on one would get hurt. She looked at each piece, they were like her dreams all shattered. No amount of glue could put them together again. A piece of glass went into her finger and blood started coming out in a trance Rajani looked for a bandaid and put it on her finger.

Why did it hurt so much, was it just a piece of glass or was she hurting somewhere else in her body? A drop fell down and Rajani realised it was her tears which were falling down. Telling Sandy just a minute she went to the bathroom put the cup on the sink and burst out crying. Why was she crying? Why was her heart hurting so much? Why couldn't she breathe properly?

After all it was just a glass piece not that her bone was broken or anything.

Rajani sat down on the floor of the washing room and cried her eyes out, really sobbing now till there was banging on the door. Sandy was yelling; "are you planning to come out today or your majesty will be inside the whole day?" Quickly Rajani washed her face and came out with a smile pasted on her face. She would never give anyone the privilege of to anyone to see her crying this way. No she was stronger than this! What a big mistake Rajani was making she had no idea.

She came out and saw her sister in law Sandy standing there. Will you make the soup for my mother or will you let her die of hunger? What about my father? Rajani felt like slapping the face in front of her, inside her heart came the scream: you bitch, what don't you get up off your ass and make something for them? But the words never translated through her mouth. She just said, "I am going to" and went ahead and did just that. She made the soup and dished something for her father in law and then started on a third kind of food that the family would have.

She went to get the laundry, started the washing machine. The noise from the machine seemed to bury down her voice which wanted to scream, yell and tell everyone to get out. Like always Rajani kept the voices buried inside her. Not saying a word to anyone and who was there to ask really? No one.

Shivam and Rajani had to move to another room, which was a study, plus gets a few carpets to make a bed and slept on them.

So the siblings, mother in law has to be near the bathroom fair enough because mother in law was sick. So Aisha would sleep with her. The kids were in one room and mother in law in the third.

So Shivam and Rajani slept on the floor, many a times Rajani would get up in the middle of the night and her whole body aching would go to the kids bedroom take arya out of her crib and put a comforter on her. She lay down by her side humming a lullaby. This was the comfort zone. Almost instantly, Arya knew her mother needed comfort and snuggled up to Rajani finally allowing sleep. Her aching body finally found the balm that the kid's room offered.

Rajani was a very strong woman but something inside her seemed to be cracking down. It was as if her heart was getting broken piece by piece and her mind wanted to just stop thinking.

Rajani's childhood was filled with a houseful of cousins and friends. Rajani's life was full of cousins from both maternal and paternal relatives.

Rajani's childhood would not be complete if she left out her cousins who were a big part of her life, and still there to support each other.

Rajani lived in a house, which is in between most of her cousin's houses. After classes, the older cousins who were in college came to their house. The house was full of 4 or 5 cousins besides the family. Her mom, the most beautiful person would make fresh snacks for all of them. The clan of 7 to 10 cousins wiped away the amount of what is known as samosas.

Not a single frown on her stunning face with the red bindi.

We all ate together. We played hide and seek. That is when you make the room dark than one person has to find others in the dark room. We managed to change clothes with each other in the dark so we could not be found. One day we were all playing in the dark bedroom. In those days houses used to have open ledges to store stuff-now they have enclosed them. So my cousin Vishnu managed to climb up on the ledge to hide there.

The room was completely silent when rajanis mom burst the door open to inform my cousins that the car had come to pick them up. Now rajanis mom opened the door in the complete darkness Vishnu jumped from the ledge to landing on the bed on the floor. Vishnu jumped in a hurry and the force of him landing on the bed cracked the bed in two. In complete silence with the open door, the bed cracked into half and we we all looking at the door.

The best part of that incident was that no one pointed fingers and said he or she did it. We were all part of the same whole, so when someone made a mistake we all hung our heads down.

A minute of complete silence all eight of us looking at the broken bed. Then Durga burst out laughing and then all of us were laughing out loud and clear, rajanis mom joined in the laughter. The consequence was we had to clean up the room getting the broken bed out of the room. No one delegated duties to the other one then. It was quite common that the elder ones took the broken bed out and the younger ones took the pillows and folded the sheets.

The cousins left for their houses.

It was upon us, as it would mean that one of us sleeping on the floor for at least a week while the bed was being made. Durga supervising to make sure it was stronger than the one before.

In all Rajani had a total of 10 or 12 cousins and they are a very big part of her life.

Pratap was quite a character. He was the rebel in the family. His parents wanted him to become a doctor. It is worth mentioning that each of her cousins shaped her to be the person she became.

The family is full of MBAs, Drs, Engineers, as well the little girl Dominic A there are molecular family the straw because you need meeting you stupid it as IAS and IFS. Indian administrative service, Indian foreign service etc.

They are a bunch of highly educated people no one is without a masters degree at least. Most have PhDs.

Pradeep was very intelligent but was a rebel. He loved his favorite pair of jeans which no one was allowed to touch until it got washed. Rajani was a cleanliness freak. Even the curtains were washed regularly in rajanis childhood home.

Rajani' s mother never interfered with it even though it was being done in her house. She was like let them do what they want as long as her children and her husband were not affected.

One day when Pratap was out his mother decided to wash his favorite pair of jeans. When Pratap came back, he was looking for his favorite pair of jeans, which was hanging like a person given a death sentence. Pratap was full of anger he knew who had done it. He marched very much like a soldier taking all his mother's clothing, which were neatly folded and threw them all in cold water. My aunt was shocked beyond belief and looked at her clothes now lying in cold water and the hanging pair of jeans. She knew to keep quiet and go into her room.

My cousin Pratap not yet satisfied went to her room banging it open and gave his mother a long speech. We all heard it but kept quiet in our room giggling at the situation.

My aunt was on a second mission. Now she wanted him to become a Dr of course. Pratap being the rebel wanted to do what he was interested in. He went for the exam and spent 3 hrs leaving each page blank

He stood for all India Banking exams and passed out with flying colors

The next time Ragani visited India he handed her Rupees and said this is all the Rakhis he had missed giving her. That money was priceless for Ragani that she brought a small silver Ganapathi from it.

The statue still sits in her Temple remimiding her of him. The bond between a brother and sister. Pratap passed away at a very young age. He got up one morning and made tea for his parents, took out his clothes for the day and told his wife Rekha he felt strange she called the on Campus doctor who advised to take him to the hospital right, his brother Rakesh came running and took him to the hospital but it was too late, Pratap had breathed his last in the car on way to the hospital. Now they had for his daughter Ashima to fly from Mumbai to Delhi. It must have been the longest flight for her because they never told her that her dad was in the hospital not that he was Gone.

Ragani has seen so many young deaths in her life that it matured her beyond her age.

Ashima

The young daughter of Pratap, Ragani admired her from way she handled the entire situation. It is never easy to father pass away, but she did.

Ashima handled all the financial situation so her mother never had to ask for anything from anyone. She bought a house in India for a mother. Rekha bhabhi has not have to ask for anything from anyone. Ragani admires Ashi for she become from a young girl to a woman very fast, God and circumstances did not give her the time to enjoy her young years but grow up she did. In a few months.

She was working in an international company her seniors were very impressed by he **work**. Soon marriage proposals started coming for her. So, Manu who had been asking for her hand for two years now had to go through the screening from her aunts and uncles it was hilarious it might I seem it might seem to anyone in USA or other countries. In India getting married is approval of uncles and aunts and long list of relatives.

It is almost like a comedy event in which each one has their input. So after a month with everyone's approval she the long Big Fat Indian wedding. Ashima did get married (her condition was her mother Rekha would live her). So, this brave girl Ashima entered the next chapter of life being someones wife, someones daughter in law is not an easy task.

Ashima's who life changed.

Ragani could not attend the wedding, her kids were too young and to leave and travel to India was not possible for her.

Life is strange ways on how things turn so after a few years who comes to visit Ragani Ashima of course. In the midst of Wisconsin winter. Manu had to go some training course and that was in Chicago for a month. Ashima stayed with Ragni one whole. Wrapping herself in two three blankets, she often asked Ragani how can anyone lhe it new the book going down she did not learn to fly that makes blinding morning letters it exported again the there shine you in the loop on Michael everyone Richard leather got read chapter development needs it whether to the learning moment mechanical 50 minute of media events running death of you for all the Iraqis that I missed minutes which were busy jamming and empathy. Lopez recommended plus and Anke Y Eric the plastic laminate Jean the article Deuteronomy of the group would you like it limited number two brothers I started remembering him are you getting bored. What a winter it was sow ice you ask for it and Wisconsin has it.

It is October and the first snow showers in winter. The trees look beautiful with the trying to get up when she felt the soft hands of her daughter and the big warm hand of Dr rao pressing into her shoulders. Bothe of them giving her their hand to get up Ragani decided to let herself be loved and indulged this time so taking both the hans sh got up. They both looked her and smiled, regain smiled at the back. Holding both the hands she stood up and they all went inside the house. The house had a smell. Then she realised they had cooked for her. She looked up at Dr. Rao, he was holding a spoon with rice he had made for her. She took a bite and it was good. Aarya began to talk about a boy she was getting to know and really liked. Ragini could help but roll her eyes and think here we go again with a smile from ear to ear. As a tear rolled down her cheek both Dr Rao and Aarya look at one another excusing eachother of making her cry. She look at both of them this tall handsome man and sweet young daughter. Little Aarya with her beautiful big black eyes and wild thick hair. Aarya says don't worry mom I will never get married. Aarya says its time for mom to rest. She led her to the bedroom to lay down. And soon she was back at the door with saffron milk. She was acting so grown up fluffing pillows for her mother and drawing the covers.

Ragani asks both of them to sit with her. One side was Aarya and the other Dr Rao. Ragani broke into a smile and told them my dears I am only crying happy tears. the laughter of Dr. Rao, Ragani and Aarya field the house Aarya always Ragani would never say no to her. So she curled up with her mother.

Dr. Rao rolled his eyes then kissed Ragani on her forehead. Gathered a pillow and blanket and headed to the guest room to rest.

THE AUTHORS NAME IS RITA. A BOOK AUTHOR OF MASUM ZINDGI rayi (Seasons of life) was published in India in 2005. She traveled to the USA when she was a spirited young lady who loved fiction and poetry. She had lived and seen the changing time. Her growth from a child to a young mother had matured her. Ritu was a capturing personality with a passion for writing. Her message to everyone is to fly as high as you can. This book she learned to fly again is fiction.

Printed in the United States
By Bookmasters